ORLAND PARK PUBLIC LIBRARY

3 1315 00309 0466

P9-CCU-159

SEP   2000

DISCARD

ORLAND PARK PUBLIC LIBRARY
AILEEN S. ANDREW MEMORIAL
14760 PARK LANE
ORLAND PARK, ILLINOIS 60462
349-8138

DEMCO

E
FRE

For Mia, who taught me how to count to eleven. S.F.

Copyright © 2000 by Play With Your Food, LLC.
All rights reserved. Published by Scholastic Press, a division of
Scholastic Inc., 555 Broadway, New York, NY 10012. Scholastic,
Scholastic Press, and associated logos are trademarks and/or
registered trademarks of Scholastic Inc.

Book design by Erik Thé
Photography by Nimkin/Parrinello

Library-of-Congress catalog card number: 99-33396
ISBN 0-439-11014-9
10 9 8 7 6 5 4 3 2 1   0/0 01 02 03 04

Printed in Mexico   49
First edition, April 2000

One Lonely Sea Horse

ARTHUR A. LEVINE BOOKS

AN IMPRINT OF SCHOLASTIC PRESS

NEW YORK

1

Beneath the ocean, deep and wide,
One lonely, drifting sea horse cried,
"In all the cold and salty sea
I'm all alone — there's only me."

Her name was Bea, and Bea was blue
And as she cried her sadness grew.

"We'll be your friends! You're not alone!"
called two small crabs by a big round stone.

2

Three puffer fish came from behind.
"We'll join you too, if you don't mind."

3

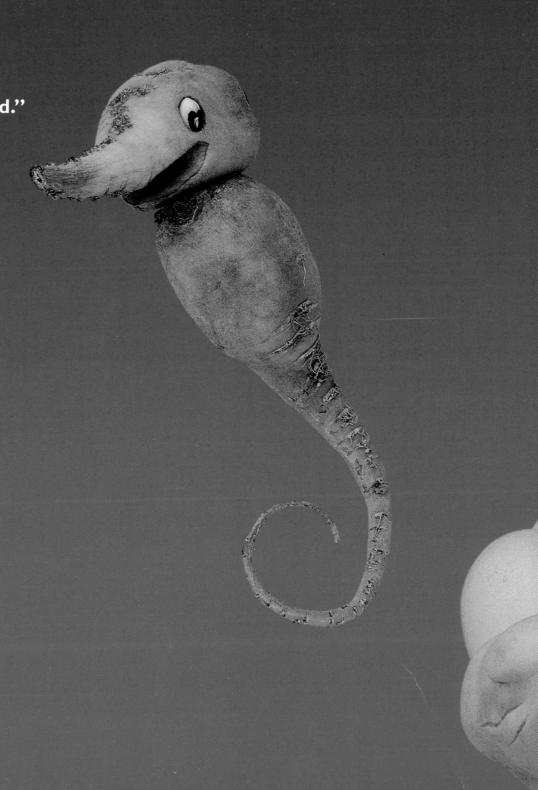

4

Four lobsters down below called, "Hey!
You're our pal too!
Come on, let's play!"

3090466

Five turtles circled Bea to say,
"Can we help out in any way?"

5

Six playful dolphins then arrived.
"Hey, Bea!" they called. "Let's leap and dive!"

6

Seven eels said, "What a shock
you're so unhappy. We should talk."

7

8

An octopus said, "We're here too!
All eight of us have hugs for you."

Nine mackerel then came swimming by.
"You feel lonely? Tell us why!"

9

10 A school of angelfish appeared.
Ten little voices laughed and cheered.

"You are my friends," said Bea, "that's true,
And I can always count on you!"

ORLAND PARK PUBLIC LIBRARY

chioggia beets

shiitake mushroom, tamarinds

horned melon

ginger

asian eggplant

red pepper

potato

lettuce

morel

cantaloupe

kale

hen-of-the-woods mushrooms

celery root

oyster mushroom

oyster mushroom

oyster mushroom